In der Fremde sprechen die Bäume Arabisch

Translated from German

In Foreign Lands, Trees Speak Arabic
Usama Al Shahmani

Translated from German by
Rachel Farmer

First published in English by Strangers Press, Norwich, 2022
part of UEA Publishing Project

First published in Switzerland by Limmat Verlag as *In der Fremde sprechen die Bäume arabisch* in 2018

All rights reserved
Author © Usama Al Shahmani, 2018
Translator © Rachel Farmer, 2022

Printed by
Swallowtail, Norwich

Series editors
Nathan Hamilton & Lucy Rand

Editorial assistance
Lily Alden, Erin Maniatopoulou and Emma Seager

Proofread by
Senica Maltese

Cover design and typesetting
Glen Robinson (aka GRRR.UK)

Design Copyright © Glen Robinson, 2022

The rights of Usama Al Shahmani to be identified as the author and Rachel Farmer to be identified as the translator of this work have been asserted in accordance with the Copyright, Designs and Patents Act, 1988. This booklet is sold subject to the condition that it shall not, by way of trade or otherwise, be lent, resold, hired out, stored in a retrieval system, or otherwise circulated without the publisher's prior consent in any form of binding or cover other than that in which it is published and without a similar condition including this condition being imposed on the subsequent purchaser.

ISBN: 978-1-913861-44-5

In Foreign Lands, Trees Speak Arabic

UEA
PUBLISHING
PROJECT

strangers press

**Usama
Al Shahmani**

Translated by
Rachel Farmer

THE TREE OF LOVE

THE FIRST TIME I HEARD THE WORD 'hiking' was in 2002. It was in May, shortly after my first birthday in Switzerland, when I met Mrs Wunderlin, the aunt of my friend Bilal, who lived with me at the hostel. She dropped by to visit her nephew, a young Iraqi who had come to Switzerland at the end of 2001, six months before I did. The aunt, who was in her mid-fifties, was the image of a Swiss woman: slim, wearing minimal makeup and simple attire, and able to talk about the things she loved as if they were important and appealing. But she had hidden sadness in her dark eyes as she recounted her hazy memories of a lost childhood between Baghdad and Qurna, a small town in southern Iraq. 'I was born where the Euphrates and the Tigris meet and are bound together for eternity,' she would say proudly. She had never been back. Even her use of the language had audibly changed in the four decades she had spent away from home. But she was still an Iraqi, through and through.

So I thought she was joking when she told us she went hiking practically every weekend. I found the whole idea incomprehensible. Setting off on foot — into the forests, mountains, valleys, along difficult paths, just for the sake of walking...

'Because your husband is Swiss?' asked her nephew.

She lifted her gym bag onto her lap and laughed. 'No. If anything, because I love it and need it.'

I was doubtful. I couldn't think of any conceivable reason why anyone would enjoy hiking.

'You should join us sometime. I could bring some Iraqi food. The best thing about hiking is the picnic.'

I declined without a second thought. So did Bilal. Wandering in the woods wasn't for him, either. 'You think I'm crazy, Auntie? You're asking me to get out of bed at seven o'clock on a Sunday morning so I can walk around some forest? As much as I love your food, I'd much rather eat it here in comfort, in front of the TV.'

I didn't understand what Mrs Wunderlin even meant by 'hiking'. Was it a sport? A hobby? I searched for an equivalent word in Arabic. I drew a blank.

'You're sure there isn't one?' she asked, sceptical.

'We don't hike. We walk, run, stroll... we saunter. Those are everyday things we Iraqis don't really enjoy doing either. But hiking? Too far. That we cannot do. Maybe for religious reasons, I suppose. There are Muslims who pilgrimage to Mecca on foot. Either because they want to perform this ritual the traditional way, as it would have been in the time of the Prophet, or because they have no money. But no. No one walks long distances otherwise.'

'That's a shame,' she said. 'You're missing out.'

Her answer astonished me. How could she forget her old home like that?

✳

That evening, Bilal kept bringing up the subject. 'Can you imagine, Usama? What would my mother say if I told her that her only sister has learnt to hike and has almost forgotten her own language?'

'How was it last time you stayed with her?' I asked Bilal.

'It was good. She cooked for me. We went to the cinema. She wasn't as cold with me as last time. But I was still mostly quite bored. Mainly when she talked about the situation in Iraq.'

'How come?' I asked.

'She always talks as though she knows more about it than I do and passes off any old allegations or lies as her own opinion. In her eyes, Iraqis are somehow responsible for what happened. At one point she even said, "We are victims of a situation for which we only have ourselves to blame."'

'When did she leave?'

'I don't know exactly. I think it was in 1975, when most of the Communists left the country. I was only one year old. My mother told me.'

'So she never experienced what things were really like under Saddam; she saw it all via the media?'

'You know what else bothers me? She talks about things that aren't important. For instance, she asked about the cockroaches and whether they're still big and in all the toilets. She was always scared of the cockroaches in Iraq, apparently. "Trust me, Bilal, the cockroaches in *Switzerland* are *tiny* and they never attack me..." she said. "Yes." I said. "Cockroaches are different here." Her husband was silent the whole time, but when she mentioned cockroaches he laughed out loud. He doesn't like me. And I don't like him. Even though he was laughing, I could tell his soul was in tatters.'

'Don't be mean, Bilal. He's helping you learn the language.' I meant it ironically, though I felt envious too.

'Yes, and he spent the whole time preaching at me about the power of language. You know, Usama, don't get me wrong. I love my aunt. Sometimes she feels like a mother to me. And she is like my mother on the surface. But it gets on my nerves. Especially when she walks around the house half-naked or kisses her crusty old husband at the table.'

'That's normal here, Bilal. We're not in Iraq anymore. You need to cast some old customs aside. Make room for new ones.'

'Even so. For me some things will never change.'

'Of course. I feel the same way. Our home still lives in us. I fled from it, it didn't flee from me.'

※

Some time later, I thought — why not try this hiking thing out for myself? I was depressed; space was tight and we were running low on almost everything. The residents of the hostel were all tripping over one another, and everyone was grumbling. But, I thought to myself, I was free to go for a walk.

I didn't have the right kit. I didn't know at the time, but, in Switzerland, every pair of shoes belongs in a certain category. My only pair of shoes were 'casual' ones. But my way into Baden from a nearby village led me through the woods. Nevertheless, on the way, near a little hut, stood a tree with a broken trunk. I thought to myself, look, its trunk is broken, and yet it's standing there proudly, its vibrant green radiating beauty. How did it stay standing so, yet forever branching out? I wondered. Did it come from its roots, or the earth in which it grew? What were roots anyway? Do us humans have them too? Could I definitively say I was an Iraqi? And what would change if I weren't? I took pleasure in this beautiful tree. I didn't care whether its roots were in Europe, or Asia.

In Iraqi culture, forests are associated with uncertainty — stories of evil spirits and demons. Palm forests are murky, unsafe places. You can get lost in the forest and not be able to find your way out. We love trees, but we detest the woods.

Most of the trees in the Swiss forest felt alien to me, apart from a few that stood in a neat line — like words clustered in a short poem. They were as familiar to me as old friends. They formed a community, like true love.

I don't know what moved me to speak aloud to them. Was it their impressive appearance? The huge linden in the centre seemed like the mother, and in the silence beneath the canopy, I spoke to it in Arabic: 'hob'. An echo came back to me, not as 'love' in German, but in Arabic. Amazed, I went on: semah... shejar... sky... trees.

Hob... semah... shejar... The Arabic echo sounded different when it came back out of the woods — thinner, sharper.

It was a lovely feeling, to hear Arabic from the woods. Nature wasn't mute, after all. You just had to talk to it and listen. The trees in foreign lands even speak Arabic, I said to myself, and opened my arms wide. I soaked up the scent of the trees, observed the branches and the buds, and felt the forest accept me as its own. I felt as though I knew the way, flouting the signposts, and I lost my bearings. Even so, I was never afraid of being unable to find my way home.

In Iraq, I never went into the woods. The images of trees and forests in my head came from stories my grandmother told me. I grew up in cities with few green spaces. Apart from private gardens, you only saw trees in the fields outside the city.

Our native trees — date, olive, pomegranate and lemon — are planted and tended by hand. Trees in the wild grow differently, as my former professor of modern Arabic poetry always insisted. Her love of nature and trees was as passionate as her love of poetry and short stories.

'The most beautiful verses of poetry are those that reflect nature, and to keep the spirit of a good poem alive it must be learnt by heart,' she used to say.

She was very fit, both physically and mentally, and spoke about poets and writers as if she knew them personally. She had a huge impact on the class. Many of the students were in love with her, myself included. She was beautiful, open-minded, liberal, single, and had a strong personality. Such a personality inspired not only respect but also a certain wariness, especially among men. Her self-confidence made her unpopular among the professors. Strong women, no matter their social class, are viewed with disdain in a society that prefers women who cannot get by without the help of a man. And the war weakened the position of women further, taking away even more freedoms.

This professor felt like the antidote to such ideas. She once told us, 'Whenever I felt stifled at home as a child, I would go into our garden barefoot and break twigs off the pomegranate tree. I still do the same today, because, for me, the best medicine for bitterness is being close to trees. These days instead of playing with the twigs, I use them to write short poems in the earth.'

'Why pomegranate? Don't you have other trees?' one of the students asked.

'Yes, we have others, but for us the pomegranate tree is the tree of love. You should know that,' she said, and began packing away her books.

I knew this, too; my grandmother had told me the same once. Every pomegranate tree has many pomegranates hanging from it but just one of them − a single one − contains a very special seed. That seed belongs to paradise, and whoever tastes the seed will be blessed with love, joy and happiness.

'Never share a pomegranate with anyone, my son, because you never know if you might be giving your love away,' my grandmother warned me.

'Have you ever found the seed?' I asked her.

She laughed. 'When I was very young, I talked about love with all the girls in our village. We laughed and giggled, but whispered only half of our secrets.'

'OK, but did you find the seed? How did you meet Granddad?'

My grandmother told me she met her husband for the first time at their wedding. Back then, girls were not permitted to meet the groom before their wedding day, she said. 'I could see him through the window when his father came to the house with him. They asked for my hand in marriage.'

It was a sunny winter's day. She had my little sister on her lap, gently stroking her hair. She went on. 'I cried that night. I was afraid because he looked like the trunk of a date palm. I didn't want to marry him. My mother tried to convince me that a powerful, strong man brings happiness in life. She told me I should press my foot down onto my new husband's right foot on the wedding night. Then I would always have the last word in our household.'

'You do have the last word! Did you press down hard?' I asked in amazement.

'No, I never got round to it.'

'And did the marriage make you happy?'

She folded her hands thoughtfully and looked at me for a moment.

'I don't know if I was happy, my love. I simply got married.'

She hadn't known happiness, yet always exuded love and lightness and wore a gentle smile. She was like a sunflower; turned naturally towards the sun. Every encounter with her was like a fresh start at enduring life in Iraq. Not much is left of her. The house in which she lived for half a century, with my grandfather and their eight children, was sold. The new owner tore it down to make way for a car wash. On my last visit to Iraq, I realised none of her more than forty grandchildren could tell me anything about her or share a personal memory. How can it be that a person who loved everyone so much left no trace of themselves behind, not even a photo?

That there were no pomegranate trees in this forest didn't stop me from doing the same: I tried to copy my professor and used branches to write in the earth. I swept the fallen leaves to one side and wrote a short poem:

> *I am the foreigner.*
> *I have hope*
> *and a suitcase full of secrets.*
> *I carry both and walk,*
> *like a Sufi, patiently*
> *trying to bloom wherever*
> *the Lord has planted him.*

※

I was comforted by the thought that whoever might read these lines would likely feel a little foreign, too, on encountering my Arabic script. Can you feel like a foreigner in nature? I wondered. In that moment, I felt an overwhelming sense of love, of belonging.

THE TREE OF HOPE

'**I CAN GIVE YOU WORK RIGHT NOW,** but I can't guarantee anything long term,' said Delshad, a Syrian-Kurdish restaurant owner born here, in Switzerland. His green eyes, slim, pointed nose and pale skin would have suggested he was native Swiss and, from a distance, his pizzeria looked as if it were made from Lego bricks stuck together by a child: squat and colourful. He worked the dough while talking to me. He was a pro, rolling the ball into a flat full moon while simultaneously answering every phone call and taking orders, the phone clamped between his ear and shoulder as he shaped the pizza base.

Often only German speakers could understand his Arabic because he spoke it with German word order. He swapped the syntax around and would say things like "kabira pizza" instead of "pizza kabira" for "large pizza". And he never started his sentences with a verb as we do in Arabic. I understood him fine, though.

'Bilal said you were looking to take on someone permanently??'
'You can start in the next few weeks. I'll explain what you'll be doing in a moment. Give me your ID. I need to make a copy and send it to immigration so I can get a permit. What's your status?'
'N.'
'Does that mean you're allowed to work?'
'Yes, I asked the head of my hostel. I'm allowed to apply for jobs. But all I'm getting are rejections. Do I need to apply here too?'
'No, no. I'll just make a copy of your whatsit. But I should tell you, I can only pay half the hourly wage — until I get the permit. OK?'
'Yes, OK. Why only half?'
'Because you're waiting for the permit. This process costs me money, too.'
There was silence as he worked the copier for a moment. 'So. To start with, you'll be putting pizza flyers through people's letterboxes in Bremgarten and the surrounding area — around ten kilometres. I'll print you out a map and I'll cover your travel. Do you have a half-fare card?'
'Yes.'
'Good, I'll give you ten francs an hour. I'll call you when the printers are done with the new flyers, so maybe at the end of the month.'
On the way back to the hostel, I looked at both sides of the sample he had pressed into my hand. The pizzas were anything but appetising. The red reminded me of a massacre.

※

Back in our room, Bilal asked why I was so agitated.
'No reason.' I replied, biting my fingernails. 'Everything's fine.'
I never normally do it and don't like it when other people do either. It's not the first time I've found myself chewing on things, however. When we were little, we didn't have many clothes. Some faded because they had been washed so many times, particularly the ones we wore at home, like our pyjamas and the floor-length white shirts we call 'dishdasha'. We would chew the hems to shreds.

I was terrible for it, especially when I was sitting beside my father. He would scold me, saying, 'If you destroy that shirt, you won't be getting a new one.'

At least my nails would grow back.

Bilal was in the process of writing a letter.

'What are you writing?' I asked him impatiently. He had been working on it since the previous evening. He wanted to stop his brother in Lebanon making the perilous journey across the sea.

'I need to convince him life in the West is more complicated than he imagines. He needs to wait and think very carefully before putting his life at risk. He should stay where he is. Even if he has to eat out of bins to survive,' he said, emphasising every word.

'But you're his only hope,' I said, though I understood all too well how desperate Bilal felt, and what was motivating him. We couldn't offer what we didn't have ourselves. We had no work, no money; our own lives were too much for us.

'You know, I sometimes wish all this would just turn out to be a bad dream. I don't want my brother to experience this misery here, you know?'

'I know. But what would you do in his position? You left, didn't you?'

He didn't answer. After a few minutes, I noticed we were both looking in the same direction: out of the window, where we could see the façade of an old church.

'By my grandmother's logic, happiness is contagious. She thought the key to being happy was to be friends with happy people,' I told Bilal.

'Do you want to stop being friends with me?' he responded, laughing.

'No, of course not. We can both be happy. We escaped. And we also have hope – that we'll be able to build worthwhile lives in this country. Just look at what your aunt has achieved. She managed to join the Swiss. She can be our role model,' I retorted.

'There's that word – role model – again. I'm sick of it. Yes, she jumped the fence. But at what cost?' he said, raising his eyebrows.

'What do you mean?' I asked.

'I mean, the fact she's such a Swiss wannabe... It's like she's renouncing her Iraqi heritage or something.'

'OK, so maybe she goes skiing and doesn't take sugar in her tea,' I said wryly, in an attempt to calm his temper.

'Don't talk nonsense. I just mean she has a different mentality. She may be nice, but she behaves strangely. Her heart doesn't beat like ours anymore. She doesn't want children, she doesn't want any contact with her family in Iraq, and she doesn't even talk on the phone with my mother all that much. And when I told her about my mother's back problems, you know what she asked, with a completely straight face? She asked me why she didn't just start swimming regularly. I mean... I held my tongue. But what an idiotic thing to say. Is she taking the piss? Does she not know what the situation is like for women right now? Does that sound *like* a "role model" to you?' he asked, wide-eyed by this point. 'And when my grandfather, *her father*, died, she didn't even come to the funeral. She just sent the family a card.' He turned his face away, refusing to discuss it any further.

I was surprised by the way he saw her. She'd just chosen to go her own way. Living in a foreign land hadn't made her bitter, like so many of her generation who were able to flee Iraq. They wear the bitterness of being outsiders on their faces like the marks of skin cancer.

Bilal and I lived with a handful of others in a small wooden lodge near Baden. Even the sprawling meadow we could look at through the window didn't help us endure our cramped quarters. For us, it was a place of suffering. Particularly in winter. But Bilal's situation was better than mine. His aunt helped him, here and there; he could always go and stay with her for a few days. I had no one.

*

I was on my own when it came to my job hunt too. Delshad's call never came. The flyers apparently weren't ready yet, and I should stop calling – that was the message he gave me, via Bilal.

In a moment of dejection, I resolved never to apply for another job. Every application sapped so much of my energy, and although I was given help, I waged a miserable war with formalities in a language that was alien to me. Generally my only reward for two weeks' work was a rejection within three days, if I received any response at all.

I tried my luck with the co-op noticeboard, where I offered my services as a helping hand for pretty much anything and everything. A week later, my advertisement all but forgotten, my phone rang. A serious voice greeted me by name. 'You placed an ad saying you were looking for work?'

This is how telephone calls work in Switzerland. And I find it even stranger that, after a few seconds of silence, they'll ask, 'Are you still there?' In Iraq, we generally don't give the reason we're calling immediately after greeting the person. An Iraqi phone call begins with small talk about any old thing — the weather, the traffic jam you got stuck in — it doesn't matter, so long as you say *something* before coming to the main reason for your call.

'Are you still looking? I have a temporary position as a labourer.'

'Yes,' I answered, without a second thought.

'Would you be available to do some work in my garden? And house? This Saturday?'

'Of course!' I responded, delighted.

'Does nine o'clock Saturday morning work for you?'

'Yes, very good.'

He gave me his address and a detailed description of how to get there. And that was it.

✺

The work wasn't difficult, though the garden was overgrown. At first, the man, at least seventy, didn't leave me alone. But he expressed himself in such clear and simple German that I understood him with hardly any difficulty at all. How wonderful it would be if everyone spoke German like that, I thought.

'Does it bother you, having the dog here?'

'Not at all. I love dogs. They are very close to us humans, in our emotions too.' I wanted to go on and tell him how I had written a short story in Arabic with a dog as the main character. 'The Day-to-day Life of a Foreign Dog' was the title. It was probably still lying in some drawer in Baghdad. I would have liked to tell the man what foreignness feels like from a dog's perspective. But my German wasn't up to the task. I sensed he would have liked to have a proper discussion with me, too, but could tell my modest command of the language would get in the way.

He didn't ask why I had come to Switzerland. This pleased me. I found the question of what I was doing in Switzerland overwhelming. Where should I start? When people asked what I was doing here, it sometimes felt like an invitation to tell them why I left my home at all.

The man showed me how to bundle up waste paper. 'See how I've done it?'

I copied what he had done.

'You don't have to do it exactly like me, just make sure the bundle doesn't fly apart.'

I wanted to do it exactly the same way he had done it.

'You know, in Iraq, either we throw waste paper in the bin, or we sell it to roadside vendors. You can buy cakes, sweets and other foods at the roadside wrapped in old newspapers. You buy two pieces of baklava and they come on a letter or part of some story or novel that you would like to continue reading.'

'And if you want to keep reading the story, you have to go back to the vendor and buy another page?' He laughed.

In Baghdad, we have a road called Al Mutanabbi where people lay out their books for sale in the street. During the embargo, many people sold their whole collections, which transformed the street into a kind of permanent book fair. A good friend of mine once wrote, 'Many thanks, my dear Shakespeare, Tolstoy, Dostoevsky and Ali Al Wardi. Thanks to you, I was able to buy flour, oil and sugar this month. My wife, who suffers from rheumatism, needs a new oven.

I don't know whether Balzac and Márquez will be able to manage it alone — should I add in my beautiful Hafez Shirazi anthology?'

Many of my friends worked on this street, as did I. A few of the booksellers helped us during our studies by allowing us to read books for free and use them as sources for our papers on the condition that we didn't leave any marks in them. In return, we helped the vendors transport their books every day.

'Now you're better at tying up the papers than me.'

'Thank you. May I ask why you keep so many?'

'I don't keep them; they just pile up. Since I've been living alone, I've been finding it harder and harder to bundle them up.'

I thought to myself that this fine house was rather large for just one person. On the balcony table were several empty bottles and a thick book cracked open somewhere in the middle. Opposite stood a tree. Pigeons cooed.

'What is that tree called in German?' I asked him.

'Fichte,' he answered. Spruce.

'It looks like a pyramid. In Arabic, it's called a tanub.'

'Tanub.' He attempted. 'Does it have any significance?'

'Yes. In northern Iraq, it's known as the tree of returning.'.

'Returning? Why?'

'It is said that birds always return to the tree where they learnt to fly. That's why many Iraqi mothers tie the umbilical cord of their newborn sons to a branch. No matter where he might one day end up, he will always return home.'

'Do you have a permanent job?' he asked abruptly.

'I don't have a job. I'm looking for one.'

'What would you like to do?'

'I have no idea. Maybe work with my hands. I can't speak German that well.'

'Not at all, you speak very well! Are you having lessons?'

'No, I'm teaching myself for now. Should I put the bundles back in the cupboard?'

'No, I'll show you.'

Together, we carried them down to the cellar. It was so full of stacks and piles of junk — metal gratings, books — that we struggled to find a place to put the waste paper.

'Perhaps I could call you again to come and help sort out this cellar,' he said, looking at me enquiringly.

'Yes, I'd love to. I could also mow the lawn?'

'What did you do before?'

'I studied literature. Back in Iraq, I was a teaching assistant at a university while working on my PhD.'

Without reacting to my answer, he said, 'Right, we're done here. Might I take you out for a coffee? To say thanks?'

I had expected more work but gratefully accepted.

'Yes, I think I have time. Thank you.'

There were three paintings hanging in his living room. A piano took pride of place. His library contained books in at least five languages. Most of the furniture was made of thick, sturdy wood.

In Iraq, we receive guests in the living room. Most families set aside the largest room in the house just for their guests. They furnish it with the finest things the family possesses. Children aren't allowed in and the room can remain locked for an entire year if no guests come to call.

Why do we isolate our guests from our real lives at home? I don't know. The Swiss don't. They let you go into the kitchen with them. Guests are allowed to help prepare the food. You can even join in clearing the table if you like.

His home had a warmth about it. He left me standing in the room and went to change his clothes. I stood there, alone, my gaze wandering to where the sun cast a warm glow over a painting on the wall. Between the books there were many small objects, animal figurines, crystals, envelopes. They reminded me of Iraq.

I had always hidden cigarettes between my books so I would be able to find them when times got tough. Every time I stumbled across one, long-forgotten, it filled me with happiness.

Why did this man trust a stranger? He had left me alone several times while I was working, among his valuable possessions. That was something I appreciated about Switzerland. People trusted each other. In Iraq, the rich owner of a villa wouldn't dream of placing so much trust in a hired worker they hardly knew. The war and the dictatorship sowed great mistrust among people. The space for trust grew smaller and smaller; suspicion became the norm. I lived in two different worlds because, outside my home, everyone believed the worst of each other, even people who did good things.

His trust and helpfulness were important to me. Even as I attempted to tie up the waste paper as best I could, uncertainly, and with shaking hands, I felt as though I were being treated as a guest, not hired help.

'If you want to use the toilet, it's there on the right. I just need to tie my shoes, then we can leave.'

He was wearing black trousers, a white shirt, and a coat. His shoes shone like a mirror. Shiny shoes have always fascinated me. You rarely see them in Baghdad. The dust blinds all our shoes, regardless of their quality. Even in winter, when it rains, they are never clean. Some of the wealthier students at the university had two pairs, one for outdoors and one for indoors.

'Sorry I kept you waiting, we can go now.'

He opened a drawer in his wall unit. I saw several hundred-franc and fifty-franc notes. He took two out and gave me two hundred francs, saying, 'Thank you very much for your hard work. You did very well.'

'That's too much. I only worked for four hours. I can't ...'

'It's OK. It's Saturday today. Take it.'

He turned to the door to indicate that he considered the money matter to be settled, and I put it in my pocket, delighted. Before leaving the room, I took one last look at the painting: a woman standing alone in a field. Behind her, an alpine panorama. The sun was just peeking out from behind the mountains and the shadows it cast over the valley made the woods appear dense.

'My mother gave it to me as a gift shortly before she died,' he said. I liked how attentive he was.

'Should we take the bus or walk? It's scarcely ten minutes to the centre.'

'I would like to walk. It's the best way to get to know a city.'

'You're right there. I lived abroad many years ago and explored many cities by walking. But it bothered me when people stared. Have you experienced anything like that here?'

'Yes, occasionally,' I said, laughing. 'There are stares that won't leave foreigners alone. Sometimes I sense a wall between me and other people. Then I tell myself that, luckily, these walls have windows and gaps in them.'

'How many of those windows have you found so far?' he asked. His eyes were wide and attentive.

'The first gap was the Aare. Its flowing waters always make me feel at home. The second is nature. Sometimes I stick my hands in my trouser pockets and go for a walk in the woods. Sometimes I turn my gaze right up to the treetops; sometimes I look at the tree trunks and try to figure out which is the oldest. I touch the bark and try to get to know them. When I do that, I can feel my fear of being a foreigner melting away. The deeper I walk into the woods, the clearer my inner voice becomes. For me, trees are not just an oxygen factory. They give me hope, too. And, of course, there are places I feel at ease, like this café in the old town...'

'Which one? Do you know the name?'

'No, unfortunately, but I can take you. I know the way.'

'Yes, I'd like that. Why this one in particular?'

'For me, the café is like a piece of Baghdad: small, traditional, and with many people of different ages, different backgrounds. Many of them talk with their hands, like me. And the serving lady, who is from Africa, has a very honest laugh.'

At the café, we drank black tea and talked about Iraq. He was against the war and was sympathetic to the people who had been forced to flee. The way he described life in exile made it seem extremely difficult. He made me feel I was living in a disaster without realising it. Later, I would understand a little better how right he was.

'My wife was also against the war,' he said. 'She was involved in campaigns and collected signatures to protest against it. Sadly without success. She couldn't stop it just like she couldn't stave off her own cancer. It ate away at her body until she died.'

'I'm sorry,' I said. In that moment, I wished he understood Arabic, because I didn't know the right words to comfort him in German.

He still hadn't asked why I left. For some people the notion of escape seemed to trigger a kind of fascination, while an emptiness spread within me. I learnt to measure out my answers, creating a clear image that left no room for speculation, but also didn't leave me feeling too exposed.

'This café is really nice. You know this town well.'

'Thank you.'

'What do Iraqis know about Switzerland? What do they imagine our country is like?' he asked.

'In Iraq, they say courts in Switzerland open their doors only twice a year because there is so little crime.'

'What a nice idea. But where did this image come from?'

'I don't know. Maybe because you have always had peace. Switzerland has never tried to invade other countries and has never taken part in a war. The war made us think that any country without a dictatorship or armed conflict must be like a fairy tale. At first, I couldn't believe that you might run into a politician on the street, just like a regular person. Our politicians believe everything between heaven and earth was created for them alone. I couldn't believe my eyes when I saw a well-known member of parliament riding her bike to work. Where are the police and the bodyguards? I wondered. In general, our knowledge of the West is from the colonial period — based around the military. Not exactly trustworthy sources. All American people, for example, shouldn't be blamed for what American soldiers do in Baghdad.'

'What about you? Do you want to stay? After the war is over?

Or is your country calling you home?'

'I don't know. If you're born in Iraq, it feels like you have two options: escape or die. But the greatest tragedy is to be neither killed nor able to escape. I was able to escape, but the two options are catching up with me.

'Do I stay in a foreign land where there is a conflict between my inner and outer self, where I am constantly changing, but where I will always somehow be "other"? I would be just like a beetle that has fallen on its back: always moving, without getting anywhere. Or do I return home where trauma is lurking round every corner? The war put up barriers between us all, and the hate between religions and ethnic groups is showing no signs of disappearing since Saddam fell. In fact, if anything, it's probably getting worse.

'For me, living in a foreign land feels like being without a soul. Not just in my everyday life, but in my head too; I sometimes feel like a foreigner in my own thoughts. I remember, when I first came here, I saw a man standing at the checkout in Migros with a slice of watermelon. I thought: Oh, watermelon is sold in slices here? I'm definitely going to starve.'

He laughed along with me and as I explained that nobody in Iraq would believe that people in Switzerland ask the waiter for permission to pay the bill.

'It's true, that is a little peculiar. May I call you again if I need you to do some more work for me, or even just to go for coffee? I know some good places you might like too.'

As he paid the bill, he spoke to the serving lady in Swiss German. They laughed at something I didn't understand. I laughed along anyway.

What a strange coincidence that the first Swiss man I worked for happened also to have lived in foreign lands. He said goodbye and gave me his hand. He looked me in the eyes and said, 'I know it's hard to make the transition – between your home and a foreign place. It takes a lot of energy. But I'm certain you have that energy, and you'll manage it. And don't forget, being different is no bad thing.'

With a few long strides, he left the café, surrounded by a kind of aura that was hard to define. I watched his retreating figure: tall, slim, wearing a coat and hat, like some character from a Naguib Mahfouz novel had hopped across a boundary and into my reality.

✹

Back in my room, I examined the paper on which he had written his address and telephone number. He had beautiful handwriting. His words in the deep black ink resembled a flock of birds. I had often watched the birds flying south across the wintry Iraqi sky. The flocks gave the local farmers a feeling of hope. They believed they were a sign of a fertile summer. The same kind of feeling came over me as I carefully folded the paper, slid it proudly into my pocket, and felt glad that I had gained at least one person's trust.

It was the second time since coming to Switzerland that I had enjoyed that feeling of being trusted. The first had been shortly after my arrival. I didn't know what time the last train from Zurich to Baden left. I was late because I was giving a reading at an intercultural event. At the tram stop, a Swiss woman asked me why I was standing there. She could speak a bit of Arabic and had been at the reading. She asked if she could do anything to help.

'I need to get to the main station. I need to catch a train.'

'But there aren't any trains at this hour. Can I drive you somewhere?'

I hesitated, then said, 'Thank you, but I don't live in Zurich, I live in Aargau.'

She was silent for a moment.

'Thank you, though. Don't worry, I'll find somewhere to stay,' I told her.

'I could drive you home. Where do you live?'

'That won't do any good, unfortunately. I forgot they lock the doors at ten o'clock.'

'Where do you live?'

'A hostel. For asylum seekers.'

I tried to make light of the situation. 'Really, it's not a problem. See the garden over there? It's a warm night. I'll wait there until morning.'

'That's not a garden. Do you really want to spend the night in a graveyard?'

On the way to her house, the car radio was playing a classical music programme. I didn't understand a word the presenter said apart from 'Bach' and 'music'.

'It was a lovely event.'

'Yes,' I replied with a cautious smile.

'I can only speak a little Arabic, so I didn't understand your texts very well, unfortunately. But I really enjoyed the melody of your language.'

'Yes, I recited some poems I wrote.'

Every time I answered her, I slid back and forth in my seat and tried to hold myself steady on the seatbelt.

'Is something bothering you?' she asked, looking over at me.

'No, no. I'm perfectly fine,' I answered, making the same movement. I felt anything but fine. I was extremely nervous. I was constantly wondering whether this young woman was married. Did she live with a man, or did she still live with her parents? How would she explain to them who this foreigner was that she was bringing home in the middle of the night?

Her small flat was on the third floor of an old building. The entrance was covered in photo portraits of various artists, actors and musicians. The passage was so narrow that two people wouldn't be able to put their shoes on at the same time. I could feel her breath as I took off my shoes.

'You can put your shoes in that cupboard there. Please excuse the mess. I rarely have guests.' She gestured for me to enter. 'There you are. Make yourself comfortable in the living room. I'll be right with you.'

I was confused. Should I sit down? Should I remain standing?

'Would you like something to drink?' I heard her call from the other room.

'Yes, a glass of water, if it isn't too much trouble.'

The only things in the living room were a sofa, two pictures, a bookshelf, and a table with an old record player. The old machine caught my attention. Was she a musician? Did she live here alone? I was reminded of many scenes from famous Arabic romance novels.

She returned with a glass of water, placed it on the table and said, 'I'm sorry, I don't have a guest room or spare pyjamas.'

'No need to apologise, I'm used to sleeping in my jeans.'

'I could offer you a t-shirt.'

'No, thank you. I can sleep in my clothes.'

She left the room in silence, and five minutes later brought me through a pillow and a jug of water, which she placed next to my already empty glass. 'Do you need anything else before I go to bed?'

'No, thank you. But could you just tell me where the light switch is?'

'Right behind you.'

She smiled and wished me good night. When she had gone, I sat still on the sofa for a moment. How strange, I thought, and wondered whether I should take my socks off to sleep.

She came back. 'Sorry, the toilet is on the left by the entrance, in case you need it.'

'Oh yes, thank you.'

I heard her bedroom door close. After two minutes, I turned off the light and lay down.

When I left her flat early the next morning, trying not to disturb her, it dawned on me that the Western culture in which I now lived really was quite different to the one I had seen on TV.

Those two people, who I never heard from again, have remained nameless in my memory but will continue to be remembered as my first employer and my first stay in a flat in Zurich. Their actions are anchored within me as a happy arrival in Switzerland. Both gave me strength and hope, but also a trust in my future in this country. But how can a person hold onto hope once it has been won? Despair is easy – it is free and available in vast quantities. But hope costs something; hope is hard work. You need to be ready to make the investment.

I miss the long, winter nights when we would visit my grandparents. At night, we would camp around the small fire pit that my grandfather had prepared outside and then brought into the room. My grandmother, always very well dressed, was the only one in the family with pale skin. She was rather short, somewhat fat, and had tattoos on both hands. You got a particularly good view of the decoration on her hands when she brought the tray with tea and biscuits over. She handed out the biscuits and was the only person who served the children first. She would throw a small piece of wood onto the fire, and seconds later the high-ceilinged room would be filled with a pleasant fragrance that still lingers in my nostrils. I think all her grandchildren know this scent. It reminds us of when she would take us onto her lap and give us a cuddle. She told us so many stories around that fire. Some of them frightened us. The greater our fear, the closer we would shuffle towards her.

Many years later, I learnt that the wood came from a lote tree. In Islamic culture, this tree is considered holy because Muslims believe that a lote tree marks the end of the seventh heaven and that the Prophet Muhammad encountered it on his ascent to paradise. My grandmother called it the 'tree of hope'. She firmly believed that this tree would bring luck and a long life to anyone who planted it. 'When you are grown up, you must plant a lote tree in your garden,' she once said to me, as she trimmed some branches.

I liked my grandmother. Her attitude towards life fascinated me. As a young boy, I often watched her kneading bread dough and knew that she didn't want anybody to talk to her. She almost always withdrew into the same corner of the room in which we cooked, ate, talked and slept. Finally, she would cover the dough with one of the same pieces of cloth that she used to cover her head when she prayed, and then let it rest in her wardrobe. It never occurred to me to ask what that silence meant — I was just used to it.

One evening after dinner at her house, she was singing and washing dishes in the large tub in the middle of the room, and I spoke to her.

'Aha, the same song,' I said and slid along the edge of the nearby bed, so I was closer to her.

'Yes, yes. Don't you like it anymore?' she replied and carried on humming.

'No, who told you that? I love your songs, but they're sad, and I don't like hearing the sadness in your voice.'

'My love, sadness is still there even when it's silent.'

'But why don't you ever sing or talk when you're kneading dough?'

'Don't you know?' she replied, astonished. 'Singing or talking while kneading makes the bread bitter.'

'Really? Is that true? Have you tested it out?'

'No, I learnt it from my mother. Talking can spoil a lot of things that we only notice later.'

That was her way. She never gave reasons for things. Even when she was talking about herself or her feelings, she would make do with few words. She was illiterate, the daughter of a farmer from a village near the ruins of Babylon. At the turn of the twentieth century, there was no school yet for her to attend. She got her wisdom from her grandmother and her father. She told me wonderful stories about deserts and heroes; she had a talent for bringing them to life. She was my first source of knowledge. Fairy tales, stories, proverbs, songs, pearls of wisdom, but also jokes – these were her gift to me as a child. As an adult, I searched for the origins of these stories and quickly realised she must have made them up herself.

Without intending to, I donned the role of my grandmother at another of my hostels, one in Aarau. On gloomy evenings, I would share these treasures from my childhood with my roommates. I even sang my grandmother's songs. One of my fellow residents thought they sounded like prisoners' chants. He was right, because the lyrics bore the burden of despair and fear, and they were sung with sighs. But they helped like a prayer or a blessing would. One bitterly cold night at the end of January 1991, we had no electricity or oil to keep us warm. We were all sitting in the kitchen, military aircraft roaring overhead, and endless shooting could be heard outside. 'May Allah keep us from being bombed,' my mother said, then began to sing one of those songs. She used it to soothe us all. Her voice was very similar to her own mother's.

I have inherited absolute hope from my grandmother. She never allowed herself to be consumed by despair. She scarcely showed any fear, even in the face of death. She seemed to trust in what was waiting for her. Quite the opposite from other Iraqis, many driven by their fear of hell. Hell is much closer to them than paradise. I still feel the warmth that flowed from my grandmother's soul, even now.

Hope usually comes more naturally to me than despair. But there is nothing more painful than longing for someone who has died. That longing makes even me lose all desire to keep hope alive. I reflected on this as I left my fiancée's house in Frauenfeld, where I had spoken at length about my grandmother. I was intending to return to Baden, but for some reason my feet led me to the small woodland nearby. It was an autumn morning, and the forest floor was carpeted in colourful foliage. The colours and shapes of the fallen leaves fascinated me.

I wanted to sit for a few minutes. I opened my shoulder bag and took out my brother Ali's most recent letter, which I had received the week before. It was the fourth time I had read this letter. The manager of the hostel had come up to me in the kitchen and told me, to my surprise, that I had a letter from Iraq. The way he said it suggested an uncomfortable question lurking beneath, and his eyes bid me understand that it wasn't good, as a refugee, to have contact with anyone back home. Later that evening, a young Afghan told me I should use a different address for my letters. 'You mustn't have your private letters sent to this address. You don't know who will read them before you. Plus, we're constantly being transferred, so you would have to give your family in Iraq a new address every three or four months.'

He was still wearing the same shirt he had been wearing when he fled Kandahar. He called this shirt his 'hope bringer.' When someone kept pestering him about it he said, 'I don't care that it has seen better days. To me, this shirt is a symbol of taking the leap from death to life. I was wearing it when I escaped Al Qaida, and it was with me throughout the whole saga of my journey to Europe.'

'God's will decided that neither you nor your shirt would die,' was the response of a religious Tunisian who had overheard the conversation.

'I don't care who decided I would stay alive. The main thing is, I took the leap with this shirt, and as long as I'm wearing it, I feel at ease.'

Ali has nice handwriting, I thought as I unfolded his letter.

Salam Usama, how are you? I hope you are well and that you are enjoying the time with your fiancée. Don't forget that the time a man spends with a woman is the most pleasant time of all. You shouldn't squander any of it. I fear that you are reading books instead of meeting with her.

Our parents are delighted you're going to marry an Iraqi Muslim. 'The important thing is that he loves her,' our sister Luma said. That's what I think too. Love is the most important thing — it doesn't matter whether she is an Iraqi or a Muslim.

First of all, I would like to tell you that I have read a lot in the past two months. Not because I wanted to, but because I couldn't leave the house. The times we are living through in Baghdad at the moment are worse than in the nineties. Baghdad has become a city where criminals can move freely. We are at the mercy of thieves, people with long beards, militias, soldiers, jihadists and other murderers. The city is suffering under the Islamic parties. Everyone is afraid of everyone: Shiites fear Sunnis, Christians fear Muslims, Muslims fear liberals, the former ruling party fears revenge, Arabs fear Iranians, Kurds fear Arabs, and everyone fears the allied troops. The American soldiers on the streets are being insanely cautious, and they kill anyone they see as a threat. Every morning, as I cross from the right to the left side of the Tigris, I take a good look at the river. It has become a normal occurrence to see a corpse floating down it, and it is also pretty common to hear someone on the bus talking about how they saw a dog eating a dead body early that morning. People are no longer interested in hearing stories of dead people they don't know. Death is spreading its arms wide through the streets of Baghdad. Just after midday, the streets suddenly become deserted, and all the shops and cafés close. An ominous hush descends over the city — a hush that consumes the soul.

On April 9th two years ago, when the first American tanks drove into Al-Ferdos Square in Baghdad, the whole world watched Saddam's statue topple. His head and torso fell to the ground. We Iraqis celebrated this: 'A new era has begun for Iraq.' We should have noticed that only the top half of that devil fell to the ground, because his legs are still standing firmly on Iraqi soil. I don't want to make you sad, you know. I just want to help you understand where I'm living right now. But my hope is still strong. It is still stronger than the will of the terrorists. Baghdad is and will remain the pearl of the Orient. I and my generation will make it shine again. I am writing you this letter from a café in Al-Rashid Street. This street is close to your heart, I know. Golden morning sunlight is shining down upon it. Many people are walking past the café. Hope is driving them to remain masters of their everyday lives in spite of everything. And now a street vendor is approaching with his cart of homemade baklava and kunafa. He is shouting: 'Baghdad's sweets are still sweet.'

Dear Usama, I think of you a great deal. I know you have your own problems abroad, but please hold fast to hope, because that's all there is. Remember the Iraqi saying you would often use: 'You want a rabbit? Take a rabbit. You want a deer? Take the rabbit.' That's exactly what my colleagues are experiencing right now. We meet in the big garden at the university and sit in the shade of the great lote tree. Many generations have met under that tree. Its green leaves have overheard many conversations.

Call me if you can. I miss your voice.
Ali, 11 November 2005

As I put the letter back in my bag, I realised I'd read it aloud, as if I had been reading it to someone. So what? I thought. No one knows me here. Nobody heard me apart from these trees.

I was sitting very deep in the forest, my back leaning against a thick trunk. It was the only tree that was still green among the autumn colours. A spruce – was that pure coincidence?

I stood up and looked for the way back out of the forest and into the city. I needed to give Ali a call today. What was that madman doing in a city that was burning ever more fiercely, where the scent of peace was nowhere to be found, replaced day by day by the stench of death? Why didn't he leave and head south, where our parents were living and the danger was less? I knew that he didn't like living with our parents; my older sister once told me on the telephone that Ali couldn't stand being in their presence since they had prevented him from having a relationship with a Christian woman. The never-ending struggle to reconcile everyday life with religion made living in southern Iraq extremely difficult. 'A clash between two eras,' Ali had once said drily.

No sooner had I left the forest than it started to rain. I went to the main post office in Frauenfeld. The phone booth was occupied by a young African man. He gesticulated as he talked, and glanced over from time to time, placating me with a smile. He didn't just speak, he practically sweated out his sentences. I could feel his every word without being able to hear any of them. He wiped the sweat from his forehead with his sleeve and there were sweat stains under his armpits.

I got hold of Ali on the first attempt, for once.

'How are you?' I asked him.

'Good. I got a translation job today. I'm supposed to translate two documents from Arabic into French,' he laughed.

'What kind of documents?' I asked.

'They're the deeds to an old house in Baghdad.'

The machine gobbled up the coins I fed into the slot with unbelievable speed.

'Listen, I want to tell you something.'

Ali carried on talking and laughing as I tried to condense my concerns into the space of five francs.

'I'm begging you, you need to leave Baghdad right away. Why don't you go south? Go, even if it's just for a month.'

'Stop pressuring me, Usama. You know I love you and I respect what you have to say, but I can't live anywhere but Baghdad. Don't you understand? I'm not involved with any of it, none of the conflicting parties or militias. You don't need to worry.'

'It's a civil war, Ali. It's not a game.'

'I know, Usama, I'm not a child anymore — I don't need to obey anyone. I can't live in the south. If I have to leave Baghdad, I'd rather leave Iraq altogether.'

I fell silent. The last fifty centimes flashed on the display.

'What? You want to come here?'

'No, not Switzerland necessarily. Just out. Jordan, Turkey, Lebanon, or anywhere outside this hole. But please never tell me again that I should leave Baghdad and go south — please.'

The machine had gobbled down my last fifty cents.

I slammed the receiver back on the hook and left the booth with a heavy heart. A young man was waiting outside. Apart from his cigarette, he was completely soaked through, but thankfully wasn't annoyed. He smiled as I held the door open for him. Something connected us; whether it was the hatred of being a foreigner or the hope for a better life, I still don't know.

What was driving me to seek out a connection to my family again and again? Why was I so hungry for details of their lives? I felt like I was carrying all the burdens and sorrows that my family was still suffering. As if I didn't have enough problems of my own.

How was I supposed to send Ali money when I still didn't have a job and hadn't received so much as a reply to most of my applications? Would it be better to break off contact with my family entirely and leave Iraq behind me for good? I thought of the first generation that had fled in the mid-seventies. As far as those left behind were concerned, they had completely disappeared; nobody knew where they lived. What was I doing wrong? Why was I so dependent on knowing what was going on back home? But the mere thought of never speaking to my brother, never hearing his voice again, crushed me.

On the train from Frauenfeld to Zurich, I decided I would find work at all costs, no matter what. Ironing, cleaning, selling falafel, harvesting potatoes, washing dishes, working on a construction site. The main thing was to be able to send money to Iraq to help get Ali out.

※

At dinner with Bilal, I decided to go back to Delshad's pizzeria.

'Can you call him?'.

'Yes, gladly.'

'How much did it cost you to get your brother from Iraq to Beirut?' I asked.

'I don't know exactly. Around two thousand dollars. My mother had to sell some furniture. And then we had to come up with more money to smuggle him from Beirut to Europe.'

'Can't he stay there and look for a job?'

'No, he doesn't have any papers so he would starve there. Do you know how expensive life is in Lebanon? More expensive than Switzerland. You should send Ali to Turkey instead.'

'I don't know. All I care about is getting him out of Baghdad. I recently heard Turkey stopped granting visas to Iraqis. They're putting Iraqi refugees in prison for three to four months, then sending them to Kurdistan.'

'Yes,' said Bilal, 'But the routes to Turkey are more open for smugglers. It's easier to get a forged passport in Istanbul than Beirut. Do you think Delshad's job will allow you to send any money back? It's only ten francs an hour.'

I said nothing, because I knew he was right. We sat for a while in silence, then he said, 'Didn't you once tell me you were giving Arabic lessons to some Swiss people?'

'Yes, I did.'

'Can't you get a bit of money in advance? Pay it off with lessons? If it's so important to get Ali out of Iraq, I mean?'

Bilal left me no time to reply, but instead asked another question. One that struck fear in me. 'Has Ali been threatened? By Al Qaeda?'

'No, no. Ali doesn't have anything to do with that. He's just a student – he has no connection to politics or any of those groups. I just want him to get out of Baghdad because it has become a city of gunmen and madmen.'

I felt that borrowing money was shameful, but Bilal's 'Money for Arabic' idea had got me thinking. You don't always need a reason for hope; the important thing is just to have it at all.

+SVIZRA is a series of eight chapbooks showcasing contemporary writing translated from the four official languages of Switzerland: German, French, Italian and Romansh. In giving equal visibility to each of the four languages, **+SVIZRA** offers a range of Swiss writing never before seen in English from a diverse group of some of the best authors living and working in Switzerland today, including National Literature Prize winning Anna Ruchat, Iraqi exile Usama Al-Shahmani and treasured Romansh author, Rut Plouda.

+SVIZRA is the result of Strangers Press' latest exciting collaboration with an international group of authors, translators, publishers, designers and editors, all made possible by generous funding from Pro Helvetia.

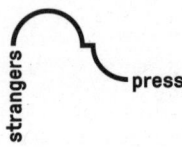

Supported By